A CENTURY
OF STORIES
NEW HANOVER COUNTY PUBLIC LIBRARY
1906-2006

Brown Rabbit's Shape Book

Alan Baker

KING*f*ISHER

BOSTON

KINGFISHER
a Houghton Mifflin Company imprint
222 Berkeley Street
Boston, Massachusetts 02116
www.houghtonmifflinbooks.com

First published in hardcover in 1994
First published in paperback in 1995
This paperback edition published in 1999
6 8 10 9 7 5 (HC)
8 10 9 7 (PB)
7TR/0305/TWP/PW/150ARM

LIBRARY OF CONGRESS CATALOGING-IN-PUBLICATION DATA
Baker, Alan.
Brown Rabbit's Shape Book/Alan Baker.—1st American ed.
p. cm.— (Little rabbit books)
Summary: Brown Rabbit finds a box of balloons and
creates various shapes from them.
[1. Rabbits—Fiction. 2. Balloons—Fiction.
III. Shape—Fiction.]
I. Title. II. Series: Baker, Alan. Little rabbit books.
PZ7.B1688Br 1994
[E]—dc20 93-29758 CIP AC

ISBN 1-85697-950-4 (HC)
ISBN 0-7534-5255-3 (PB)
ISBN 978-07534-5255-4 (PB)

Printed in Singapore

One day a package arrived
for Brown Rabbit.
It had bright red triangles
on the wrapping paper.

The card was the shape of a rectangle. It said "To Brown Rabbit."

To Brown Rabbit xxx

Rabbit took off the paper.
Underneath was a
square box. Rabbit
lifted the lid.

Inside was
a tube ...

... with a circle shape top.
Rabbit opened it.

Out tumbled
five flat floppy
balloons,
all different
colors.

Lovely balloons,
just waiting
to be blown up.

Rabbit blew up the red balloon.
It was big and round like a ball.

Whoosh! It flew off.

The orange balloon was oval-shaped like an egg.

Whoosh! Away it flew.

The green balloon was l o n g
and sausage-shaped.
Rabbit couldn't hold it.
Whoo-whoosh!
Off it went.

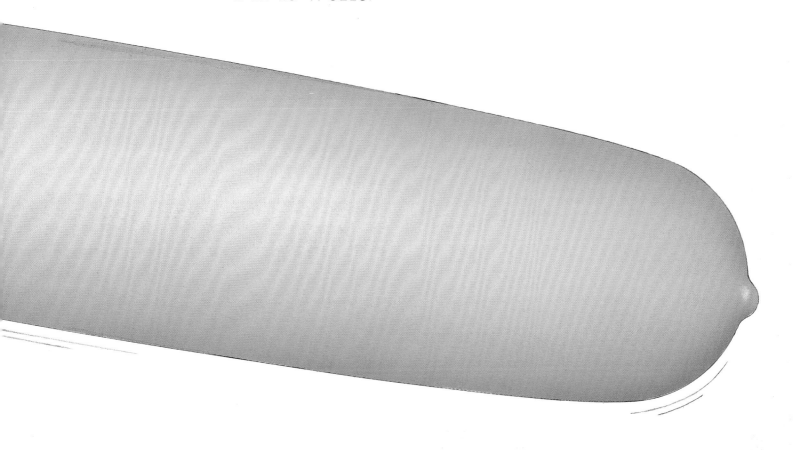

The purple balloon
was smaller and
shaped like a pear.

One more puff, thought Rabbit.
Then BANG! It burst.

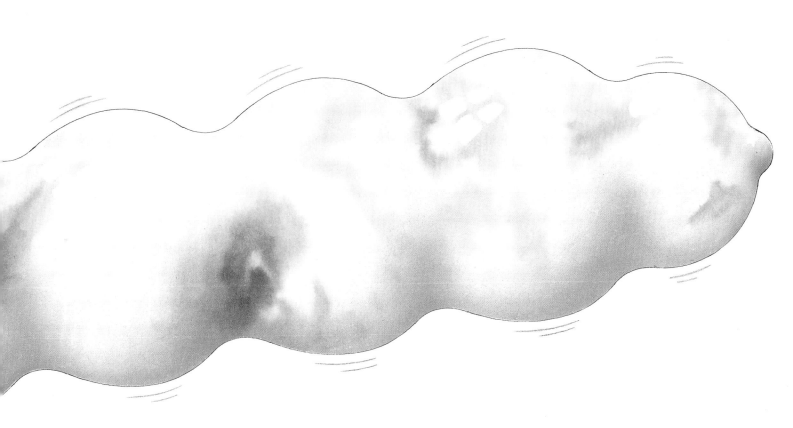

The last balloon was all colors,
l o n g and curly-wurly.

Whoosh! Blast off!

Whoo ... Whoo ... Whoo-oosh!

Goodbye, balloon shapes.
I'm all out of puff,
thought Rabbit.

He tidied up the balloons,
the tube, the box,
and the paper.

Then rabbit-shaped Rabbit
fell fast asleep on top.